ANDY THE ALIEN

A Social-Emotional Learning Story

Written by
Dave VanderMolen

Illustrated by
Becca Hart

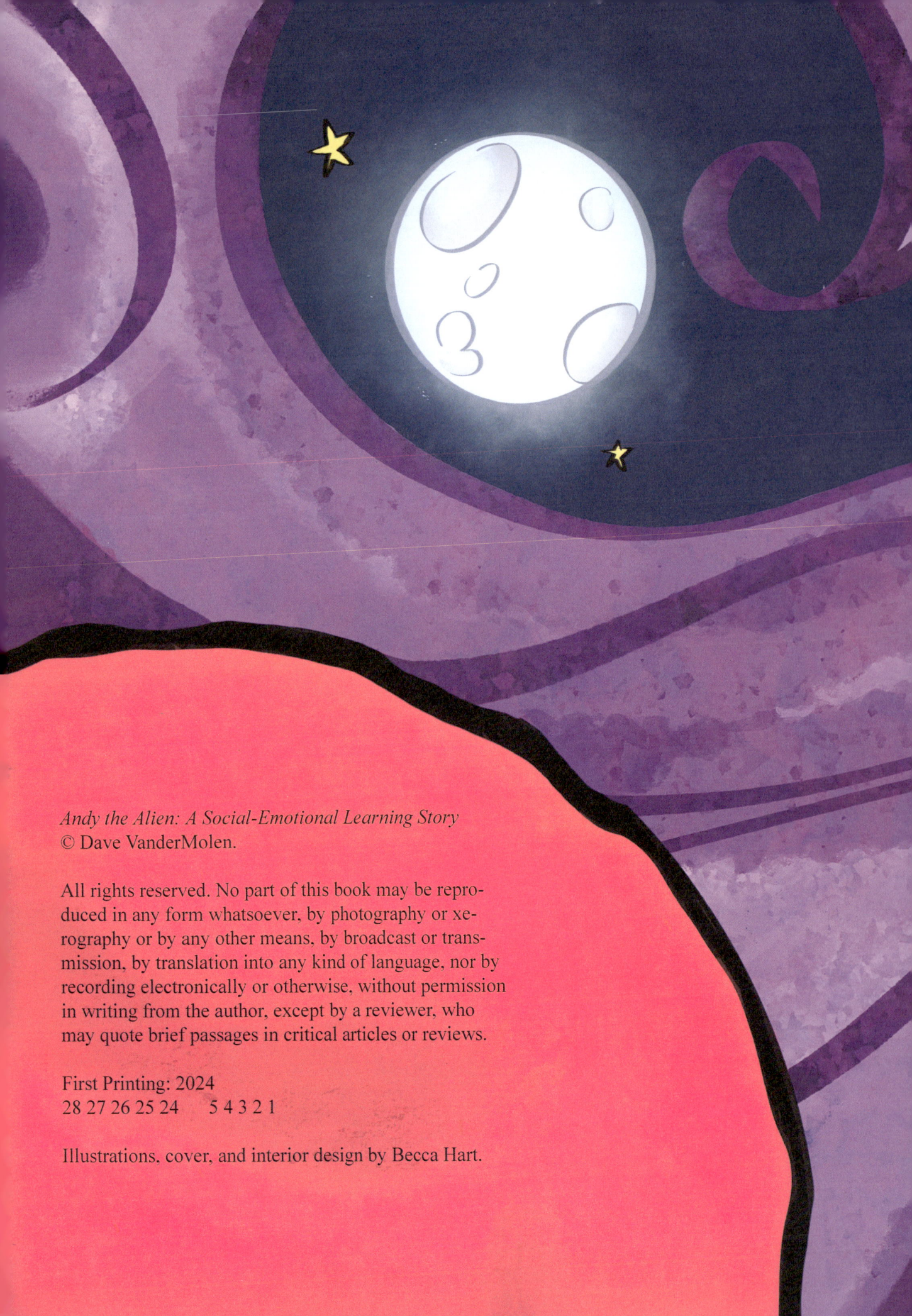

Andy the Alien: A Social-Emotional Learning Story
© Dave VanderMolen.

All rights reserved. No part of this book may be reproduced in any form whatsoever, by photography or xerography or by any other means, by broadcast or transmission, by translation into any kind of language, nor by recording electronically or otherwise, without permission in writing from the author, except by a reviewer, who may quote brief passages in critical articles or reviews.

First Printing: 2024
28 27 26 25 24   5 4 3 2 1

Illustrations, cover, and interior design by Becca Hart.

Greetings, Earthlings.
My name is Andy!

I have a special way to show how I am feeling —
the color-changing feelers on top of my head!

Humans have feelers too, but they are on the
inside of their bodies.

Where do you feel *your* feelings?

When I feel
happy, calm, and safe,

my feelers glow bright green.

When my feelers are green, I can play in the classroom with my friends and focus on learning.

What do you like to do when *your* feelers are green?

Sometimes things happen that make me feel frustrated or upset,

and my feelers start to glow yellow.

When my feelers are yellow,
I can choose a calming activity,
ask for help,
or take a break.

Doing these things will help my feelers turn green again!

Sometimes things happen that make me feel very, very mad,

and my feelers start to glow red.

This might happen when
a classmate takes something that is mine,
when my feelings are hurt,
or when my body is hurt.

What are some things
that make *your*
feelers turn red?

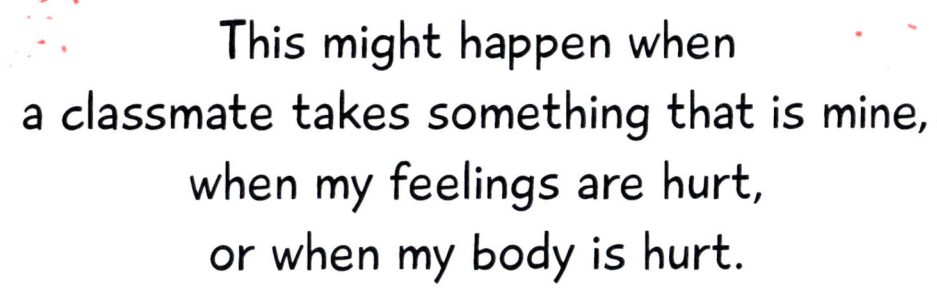

When my feelers turn green again,
I can check in with others and ask if they are ok.

It is ok to have lots of different feelings!

Remember that teachers are here to help when your feelers start changing colors.

Until next time,
this is Andy the Alien,
hoping that your day is filled with
moments that make your feelers
glow the brightest green!

About the Author

Dave VanderMolen (MA, Special Education) is a Minnesota native who has been working with students for over 15 years. His love for this work inspired him to create a story to help people navigate emotional situations. Dave first dreamed up Andy when he was in elementary school, and he is so excited to finally have the opportunity to share him with Earthlings!

About the Illustrator

Becca Hart has been drawing since she was Andy's age. Raised in Oklahoma, she moved north to study children's literature and visual art at St. Olaf College in Minnesota. Hart is the illustrator of several children's books and a graphic novel, which she created with Wonderlust Productions, *In My Heart: The Adoption Project*. For more, visit www.BeccaHart.org.

Printed in the USA
CPSIA information can be obtained
at www.ICGtesting.com
LVRC091427261023
762208LV00024B/340